Robby Novak

Kid President and Promoter of Positivity

Linda Barghoorn

Crabtree Publishing Company
www.crabtreebooks.com

Author: Linda Barghoorn

Series research and development: Reagan Miller

Editorial director: Kathy Middleton

Editor: Ellen Rodger

Proofreader: Wendy Scavuzzo

Photo researchers: Samara Parent

Designer and prepress technician: Samara Parent

Print coordinator: Katherine Berti

Photographs:

AP Photo: © Kristi Montague/Microsoft: pages 22-23; © Charles Dharapak: pages 24-25; © Jon Morgan/AP Images for ConAgra: pages 26, 27; © Scott Roth/Invision/AP: page 30

The Canadian Press: © Hub Network / Courtesy: Everett Collection: page 10, 18-19

Getty Images: © C Flanigan/FilmMagic: cover, pages 21, 29; © Stephen J. Cohen: title page, page 20; © Alex Wong: pages 6-7; © Frederick Breedon IV/WireImage: pages 8-9; © Bob Thomas: page 12; © Gemma Levine/Hulton Archive: page 13 (top); © Ralph Crane/The LIFE Picture Collection: pages 14-15; © Larry French/Getty Images for The Jefferson Awards Foundation: pages 16-17

Public Domain: pages 4-5, 28

Shutterstock.com: © Leonard Zhukovsky: page 13 (bottom)

Wikimedia Commons: © ShakataGaNai: page 11

All other images from Shutterstock

About the author: Linda Barghoorn has been sharing stories—hers and others—for years. She has interviewed rap musicians, TV news anchors, and most importantly, her dad. She is the author of several children's books and is working on a novel about her father's life.

Library and Archives Canada Cataloguing in Publication

Barghoorn, Linda, author
Robby Novak : Kid President and promoter of positivity? / Linda Barghoorn.

(Remarkable lives revealed)
Includes index.
Issued in print and electronic formats.
ISBN 978-0-7787-4702-4 (hardcover).--
ISBN 978-0-7787-4713-0 (softcover).--
ISBN 978-1-4271-2075-5 (HTML)

1. Novak, Robby--Juvenile literature. 2. Internet personalities--United States--Biography--Juvenile literature. 3. Optimism--Juvenile literature. I. Title. II. Series: Remarkable lives revealed

PN1992.9236.N68B37 2018 j070.5'79738092 C2017-907724-4
C2017-907725-2

Library of Congress Cataloging-in-Publication Data

Names: Barghoorn, Linda, author.
Title: Robby Novak : Kid president and promoter of positivity / Linda Barghoorn.
Description: New York, NY : Crabtree Publishing,[2018] | Series: Remarkable lives revealed | Includes index.
Identifiers: LCCN 2017057535 (print) | LCCN 2018008183 (ebook) | ISBN 9781427120755 (Electronic HTML) | ISBN 9780778747024 (reinforced library binding : alk. paper) | ISBN 9780778747130 (pbk. : alk. paper)
Subjects: LCSH: Novak, Robby Juvenile literature. | Internet personalities--United States--Biography--Juvenile literature. | Actors--Biography--Juvenile literature | Osteogenesis imperfecta--Patients--United States--Biography--Juvenile literature. | Kid President: declaration of awesome (Television program)
Classification: LCC PN1992.9236.N68 (ebook) | LCC PN1992.9236.N68 B37 2018 (print) | DDC 302.23/1092 [B] --dc23
LC record available at https://lccn.loc.gov/2017057535

Crabtree Publishing Company
www.crabtreebooks.com 1-800-387-7650

Printed in Canada/082020/CPC20200804

Published in Canada
Crabtree Publishing
616 Welland Ave.
St. Catharines, Ontario
L2M 5V6

Published inthe United States
Crabtree Publishing
PMB 59051
350 Fifth Ave., 59th Floor
New York, NY 10118

Published in theUnited Kingdom
Crabtree Publishing
Maritime House
Basin Road North, Hove
BN41 1WR

Published in Australia
Crabtree Publishing
3 Charles Street
Coburg North
VIC, 3058

Contents

Introduction Robby Novak 4

Chapter 1 Finding a Family 6

Chapter 2 Living with Osteogenesis Imperfecta... 10

Chapter 3 Kid President 16

Chapter 4 Making the World More Awesome 22

Chapter 5 Spreading Awesome Ideas 26

Writing Prompts 30

Learning More 31

Glossary 32

Index 32

Robby Novak

We enjoy reading about other people's lives to learn more about the world we live in and our place in it. Stories of their **resilience**, courage, or strength can inspire us. Robby Novak was born with a disease which leaves him **vulnerable** to broken bones and pain. But he refuses to let this disease limit his hopes and dreams. Instead, his enthusiasm, **optimism**, and determination have helped him make a special contribution to our world.

What Is a Biography?

A biography is the story of a person's life and experiences. We read biographies to learn about another person's life and thoughts. Biographies can be based on many sources of information. Primary sources include a person's own words or pictures. Secondary sources come from friends, family, media, or research.

Kid President Robby Novak tries the real Oval Office on for size during a visit to the White House.

What? A Kid for President?

Robby Novak is famous for a character he plays called Kid President. As Kid President, Robby wants to change the way adults see children and their role in **society**. He also wants to shape the way children think about themselves and their power to create change. Robby's dream is to **unite** kids and adults to create a happier, better world for all of us.

THINK ABOUT IT

As you read about Robby Novak, think about the qualities that make him remarkable.

Chapter 1

Finding a Family

Robby was born on January 26, 2003, in Henderson, Tennessee. He has a sister, Lexi, who is 15 months older than him. David and Laurie Novak became Robby and Lexi's **foster parents** when Robby was just two months old. The Novak's were told that both children have a rare disease called Osteogenesis Imperfecta (OI). It made them vulnerable to broken bones and frequent pain. They didn't realize how the disease would change their lives.

Foster Home

Foster parents provide a home for children whose biological, or birth parents are unable to care for them.

Kid President "rolls with it"! Robby participated in a White House Easter egg roll in 2013 with President Barack Obama and family.

A Foster Home

David and Laurie already had a family with three grown children of their own. They had not planned to adopt Robby and Lexi, but wanted to provide them with a safe, loving home. They found themselves in the hospital emergency room again and again as the children suffered one broken bone after another. Their bodies were so **fragile** that David and Laurie began to feel they could not keep Robby and Lexi safe and healthy.

> *Love changes everything. So fill the world with it.*
>
> **—Robby Novak on Twitter, July 2015**

Nowhere to Go

As time passed, David and Laurie decided they could no longer care for Robby and Lexi. But when they contacted the foster agency to discuss other options, they were told the children had nowhere else to go. There was no one else to care for them. At that moment, the Novaks decided to learn more about the disease so they could provide Robby and Lexi with the best care possible. Two years later, they adopted both children. Robby and Lexi became permanent members of the Novak family.

> *Since I was born I had over 70 breaks… but I still dance.*
>
> **—Robby Novak, *The True Story of Kid President*, video, February, 2013**

THINK ABOUT IT

What advice did Robby's parents get about raising the children?

The Novak family enjoys normal activities together, such as movies or days at the beach. Robby and Lexi's bodies are fragile, but the Novaks try not to shelter their children.

Just Like Other Kids

David and Laurie wanted Robby and Lexi to lead happy and full lives. They also wanted to protect the children from accidents that could cause broken bones. When Robby first asked for a bicycle, they said "no." Another mom who had OI, and children with the same disease, encouraged them not to be overprotective. She suggested they encourage Robby and Lexi to be **independent**. This way, they would not be afraid to try new things and could live normal lives.

Living with Osteogenesis Imperfecta

Robby and Lexi have a rare bone disease called Osteogenesis Imperfecta. It makes their bones prone to breaks. During his lifetime, Robby has had more than 75 bone breaks or **fractures** and 13 surgeries. He can name the broken bones he's had like a lesson in human **anatomy**. Robby refuses to let the disease stop him from leading a normal life and using his sense of humor to make the world laugh.

The actor Kevin Costner discusses the importance of helping others with Kid President.

What Is Osteogenesis Imperfecta?

Osteogenesis Imperfecta is also known as OI, or **brittle** bone disease. It happens when a person's body doesn't produce the material needed to form strong bones. Some people suffer only mild symptoms, while for others the disease is life threatening. People with OI can also experience hearing loss, **fatigue**, curved bones, teeth that crack or break easily, or breathing problems. Some are short in height. There is no cure yet, but medicine has been developed that can help make bones stronger and the pain less severe.

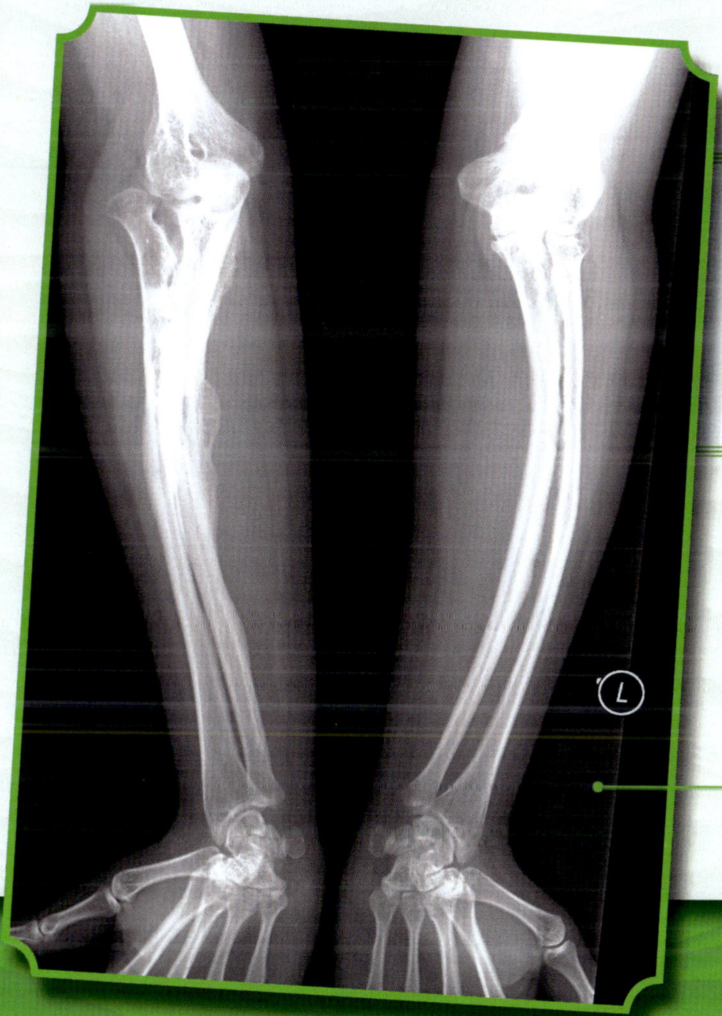

Rare Disease

OI affects from 25,000–50,000 adults and children in the United States alone.

OI can cause bones to curve as shown in this X-Ray of forearm bones.

Finding Help

Robby and Lexi will always have OI, but they now receive regular medical treatments that help them carry on with their lives. Their parents worked hard to find a doctor who could provide the proper care and medicine that helps them to get stronger.

Olympic rower Doug Herland is congratulated on his bronze medal win.

Unstoppable

OI is a rare disorder, but several famous people live with it. They have accomplished great things despite the difficulties of everyday life.

Doug Herland, an American, won a bronze medal in rowing at the 1984 Olympics.

Nabil Shaban, a British writer and actor, helps train people with disabilities to become performers.

Jordanne Whiley, a British wheelchair tennis player, has 4 Grand Slam titles and a bronze medal from the 2012 Paralympic Games.

Making Strong Bones

Robby travels every three months to receive treatments at a hospital in Nashville, Tennessee. Each treatment takes about five hours. For someone like Robby who finds it hard to sit still, five hours seems like a lifetime. He tries to keep busy with his iPad and some video games. Robby has learned to be patient and take things in stride. He will need treatments for the rest of his life. The medicine helps increase **bone density**, making his bones stronger and less likely to break.

Nabil Shaban (top); Jordanne Whiley (right)

Humpty Dumpty

Robby has defied all expectations. Doctors once thought he might never walk. But he has learned to walk and ride a bike. He dances like a pro, but he is still not allowed to do sports. He and his parents are aware that some activities are too rough for his body. Robby is a **daredevil** and loves to push the limits of what his fragile body will allow him to do. His mother describes him as "Evel Knievel in Humpty Dumpty's body."

Evel Knievel

Evel Knievel was a performer who made a career out of doing dangerous motorcycle stunts and jumps. He entertained audiences around the world.

Just Dance

Robby has sometimes been bullied because of his disease. But he refuses to be limited by his condition or let it define who he is. Instead, he wants the world to dance along with him. Robby's bubbly, contagious laugh and no-limits attitude have helped him smile through the pain and difficult times.

> *Just give the world a reason to dance.*
>
> **—"How Kid President Would Lead the World," interview with Todd Aaron Jensen, February 2015**

THINK ABOUT IT

How has Robby fought against the limitations of OI?

Chapter 3

Kid President

Robby is famous, but not because of his disease or how he lives with it. In fact, he tries hard not to talk about his life with OI. He has more important things on his mind. What Robby is famous for is a role he helped create, called Kid President.

Making Videos

When Robby was just nine years old, he began making videos with his brother-in-law and best friend, Brad Montague. Brad is married to one of David and Laurie's adult daughters. They enjoyed spending time together creating things. Brad is a filmmaker and storyteller. He realized Robby's talent for spreading joy and optimism and helped make the videos. Robby is a natural entertainer and loved playing the role of Kid President. They began by making the videos for family and friends. But the videos became so popular they decided to make more and share them with a bigger audience.

> *You were born for a reason and you have a purpose—to be awesome and do awesome things.*
>
> **—"How Kid President Would Lead the World," interview with Todd Aaron Jensen, February 2015**

Robby's brother-in-law Brad Montague is a best friend and collaborator. They work together on crafting Robby's Kid President character and video messages.

Adult versus Kid

In the videos, Robby wore a suit and a bright-red tie. Kid President dressed like an adult, but he definitely talked like a kid. He often spoke from a cardboard Oval Office, complete with a tin-can phone. His unique "Seal of the Tiny President of the United States" appeared on the back of the office, looking a lot like the real thing. Kid President's videos used humor, dance moves, famous quotes, and his own words of wisdom. The message themes were always about making the world a better place, and the videos were fun and funny. They were all from a kid's point of view, but Kid President also encouraged adults to listen.

Robby is a natural ham in front of the camera, but his messages have meaning.

A Kid's Voice

Brad made the videos with Robby because they believed that kids have things to say that are worth listening to. Imagine people listening to a Kid President? But people of all ages started to do just that! The videos make people laugh. But they also deliver important messages about how we can all act to make the world happier and more interesting.

THINK ABOUT IT

Why did Robby and Brad start making videos?

A Bigger Audience

The first video they made got 200 views. The next one got 2,000 views! That was the size of the whole town where Brad lived. Brad and Robby couldn't believe what was happening! Soon their videos became wildly popular on social media. One of the most popular videos was called *A Pep Talk from Kid President to You*. In its first week online, more than six million people watched it. Since then, it has been seen by more than 40 million people.

> *The world needs you to stop being boring.... Boring is easy. Everybody can be boring. But you're gooder than that.*
>
> **—*A Pep Talk from Kid President to You* video, 2013**

Robby is interviewed at an awards ceremony he attended.

Making the World Better

Robby and Brad did not start out to make money or be famous. They just wanted to help make the world a better place—to spread hope and happiness through laughter and dance. Robby claims he also wanted to make adults less boring by making them behave more like kids. But he especially hoped to inspire kids to explore what makes them special and to share this with others.

Robby and Brad inspired young people at a WE Day event in 2015. WE Day raises funds for charities.

Making the World More Awesome

Robby has many fans from schoolchildren to Hollywood celebrities. He asks them all: "What will you do to make the world more awesome?" Robby believes that life should be like a party where people treat others like it's their birthday every day. Imagine what a happy world we could create if every day was this special! In 2013, Robby made a video called, *The Awesome Year Challenge*. In the video, he outlined 25 ideas to help make someone else's year awesome.

Robby and Brad teamed up with computer company Microsoft in a campaign to improve learning with new school computers.

Find Your Jam

Robby is a courageous and optimistic person. He does not believe in giving up—ever! Robbie wonders what if Michael Jordan had quit basketball in high school? He wouldn't have made the *Space Jam* movie (one of Robby's favorites). "What's your Space Jam?" Robby wants to know. He asks this to encourage us to think about what unique talent each of us can share with the world. By sharing these special talents, we can make each other and the world a more positive and happy place.

Celebrating Lives

Robby uses his videos to help celebrate events in people's lives—from marriage proposals to graduations and charity projects. He also participates in events to honor others. He has helped Beyoncé promote World Humanitarian Day. This day honors **aid workers** who work with and sometimes die while helping others. He also joined former President Barack Obama in remembering a 1963 civil rights march by Martin Luther King Jr. Robby finds goodness in people everywhere.

Words of Advice

Robby shares simple but wise suggestions about making the world a more awesome place. Some of these bits of wisdom are his own. Others come from quotes by his favorite poets or leaders. He is especially inspired by a line from one of Robert Frost's poems: "Two roads **diverged** in a yellow wood and sorry I could not travel both." Robby asks: "What if there really were two roads? I want to be on the one that leads to awesome!"

THINK ABOUT IT

What messages is Robby trying to deliver to his fans?

Be Yourself!

Be who you are.

If you have a talent, show it off.

Don't be afraid to try something new.

Dance more!

Robby gave a speech at the 50th Anniversary of the **March on Washington**. *The March on Washington was a civil rights march led by Dr. Martin Luther King Jr. in 1963.*

Spreading Awesome Ideas

Robby and Brad have created more than 100 videos. Some feature ordinary people doing extraordinary things. Others feature celebrities to highlight causes that Robby feels are important. He has flirted with actress Emma Stone, kissed Beyoncé, and danced with Grover from *Sesame Street*. In 2014, Robby starred in a ten-part TV series called *Kid President:* ***Declaration*** *of Awesome*. The following year, his book *Kid President's Guide to Being Awesome* topped the bestseller charts.

Robby and country music star Dierks Bentley and family helped out at a food bank in Tennessee.

Socks and Food

Robby and Brad created a project called Socktober to encourage people to donate much-needed socks to **homeless shelters**. Soon people everywhere began to create local projects to support them. Each year Robby hopes to give away more socks than the last. That's millions of warm feet! When Robby heard that one-in-five American children don't have enough to eat, he made a video to call attention to child hunger. *Kid President Needs Your Help to Fight Child Hunger* has inspired people to act. Robby now works with several organizations to spread awareness and provide 500,000 meals to children in need.

> *The world is changed by you: one person filled with love.*
>
> **—*Kid President Gives Back to the World* video, 2016**

Kid President teamed up with a food company to give meals to a food bank and help feed hungry people.

Robby for President?

Robby once interviewed former President Barack Obama in the White House. He was even invited to try out the president's chair in the Oval Office. But he doesn't really want to be President of the United States (POTUS). He thinks it's too difficult a job, with too much paperwork. He'd like to be a U.S. **Marine** when he grows, up so he can help save the world. But for now, Robby seems content in his role as Kid President. He enjoys entertaining people and spreading his message of **empowerment** to kids.

Robby may look presidential, but he doesn't want to be POTUS. He'd rather entertain people to make the world a better place.

Shoes to Fill

Here are some ideas to help you follow in Robby's footsteps:

- **Use your voice to share your ideas and values.**
- **Organize a sock drive for a local homeless shelter.**
- **Celebrate every day like it's a birthday.**
- **Make someone feel special every day.**

Following in His Footsteps

Robby just can't stop himself from dancing. He dances when he's happy and to stay positive when things get tough. He is an amazing example of someone making a difference despite some incredible personal challenges.

? THINK ABOUT IT

What are some of the things you can do to spread kindness?

Writing Prompts

1. How is Robby a role model for other kids?
2. Has Robby's disease, OI, limited his life in any way?
3. If you could deliver one message to the world that is important to you, what would it be?
4. What do you believe is Robby's most important message to the world?
5. How does Robby work to bring kids and adults together?
6. List five things that Robby has done to help change the world.

Learning More

Books

Kid President's Guide to Being Awesome by Brad Montague and Robby Novak. Harper Collins, 2015.

How To Be A Good President: Lessons from Kids by Children of America. Wyatt-MacKenzie Publishing, 2017.

Real Kids, Real Stories, Real Change: Courageous Actions Around the World by Garth Sundem. Free Spirit Publishing, 2010.

I am Me… You, Us and We by Caroline Trowbridge. Baker-Duly Books, 2017.

Kid Presidents: True Tales of Childhood from America's Presidents by David Stabler. Quirk Books, 2014.

Websites

http://kidpresident.com
The official website of Kid President, Robby Novak. Includes pictures, links to his videos, and a note from Brad about the aims of Kid President.

https://www.ted.com/speakers/kid_president
Features a TED Talk given by Robby Novak and includes other interviews and chats.

http://soulpancake.com/portfolio_page/kidpresident/
Learn more about Kid President from the company that helps create his videos.

http://happysocktober.com
Learn more about the Socktober movement and how you can get involved.

http://kidshealth.org/en/kids/bones.html
Quizzes, videos, and fun facts to help you learn more about your bones.

Glossary

aid workers People who work for charitable organizations, helping others, especially in conflict zones

anatomy The parts that form a living being such as a person or animal

bone density The amount of bone minerals, such as calcium, found in bone tissue

brittle Something that is hard, but easily broken

daredevil A person who does dangerous things, often to get attention

declaration An official statement about something

diverged Split into different directions

empowerment To give power to someone

fatigue The state of being tired

foster parents People who take care of children who are not their own

fractures breaks

fragile Easily broken

Grand Slam A set of major championships or matches in a particular sport in the same year

homeless shelters Places that provide protection and support for people who do not have anywhere to sleep

independent Not depending on others for everything

March on Washington A famous march for civil rights

marine A member of the U.S. military force that serves on a ship

optimism Feeling or showing hope for the future

resilience The ability to recover after something bad happens

society People living together in a community with shared laws and values

unite To join together

vulnerable Capable of being hurt or injured

Index

Beyoncé 24, 26
dancing 8, 14, 15, 18, 21, 25, 26, 29
foster care 6
Herland, Douglas
Kid President 5, 16–17, 18–19, 26, 27
  book 26
Montague, Brad 17, 18, 19, 21, 22, 23, 26, 27
Novak, Lexi 6, 7, 8–9, 10, 12
Novak, Doug and Laurie 6, 8–9
optimism 4
Osteogenesis Imperfecta 6, 10–11
Shaban, Nabil 13
Socktober 27
Whiley, Jordanne 13
World Humanitarian Day 26–27